Tim
never forgets

Om
KIDZ
An imprint of Om Books International

Om KIDZ | Om **Books International**

Reprinted in 2021

Corporate & Editorial Office
A-12, Sector 64, Noida 201 301
Uttar Pradesh, India
Phone: +91 120 477 4100
Email: editorial@ombooks.com
Website: www.ombooksinternational.com

© Om Books International 2015

Content by Sonia Emm

ISBN: 978-93-84625-06-1

Printed in India

10 9 8 7 6 5

Sales Office
107, Ansari Road, Darya Ganj
New Delhi 110 002, India
Phone: +91 11 4000 9000
Email: sales@ombooks.com
Website: www.ombooks.com

Tim
never forgets

Paste your
photograph here

My name is

J I M

NEVER
FoRGeTS

One morning, the alarm rings and wakes Tim up.

"I'm late for school!" he says.
He jumps out of bed and
rushes around.

He brushes his teeth.

He bathes.

He wears his clothes.

He combs his hair. But he forgets...

...to tie his shoe laces!

Tim cycles to the shop. He pays
the shopkeeper. He counts
the change. But he forgets…
…his cycle at the shop!

Tim gets his paints out.
He squeezes them out in bowls.
But he forgets…

…to keep his dog Tony out of the room! Tony kicks the bowls of colour and spills them all around!

"Tim, you forgot your breakfast!" his mother calls out from downstairs. "Oops! I did forget my milk and toast!" says Tim.

Tim finishes breakfast and opens his craft box. He gets his shiny papers and ribbons out.
But he forgets…

...to close the box!

Tony pulls stuff out of the box.
Buttons, stickers, ribbons and
googly eyes fall all over the floor.

Tim starts to clean. He puts everything back in its place.

He washes Tony and wipes
him dry.

Tim goes to the kitchen. He gets
milk out of the fridge.

He makes a big cup of cold coffee.
But he forgets…

…to close the fridge door!
Tony drops the jam and licks
the cream.

Tim's mother comes running into the kitchen. Tony drops a few more things.

"What a mess, Tim! How can you forget everything?" says his angry mother.

The doorbell rings. Tim runs to open it. It's Tim's father. "Wait, Dad!" he says, as he runs up to his room.

"Happy Birthday, Dad!" he sings.
He gives him a gift and
the coffee.

"Wow! I love it, Tim!" says a happy Dad. Tim never forgets Dad's birthday!

Know your words

Alarm - A clock that rings to wake you up every morning.

Laces - Strings tied together to keep your shoes from coming off your feet.

Change - Money left over after buying.

Squeezes - Firmly presses.

Spills - Allows a liquid to flow over the edge of its container.

Breakfast - The first meal that you have in the morning.

Toast - Bread that is heated until it is crisp.

Knocks - Throws down.

Googly eyes - Plastic eye-like objects, usually stuck on a toy.

Fridge - A machine that stores our food and keeps it cool.